The Adventures of Skunky

Bethany Avondet

RoseDog ❧ Books
PITTSBURGH, PENNSYLVANIA 15238

RoseDog Books
585 Alpha Drive, Suite 103
Pittsburgh, PA 15238
Visit our website at www.rosedogbookstore.com

ISBN: 978-1-63764-684-7
eISBN: 978-1-63764-724-0

The Adventures of Skunky

Bethany Avondet

CHAPTER 1

The Meet / Meat Adventure

Howdy everyone, my name is Skunky. You may be wondering who I am and what kind of adventures I like to get into with my friends. Well, let me introduce myself. I am a baby racoon.... That kind of looks like a little skunk. Sometimes I can generate some smelly smells, so naming me Skunky was only fitting. Although, I think skunks are way smellier than me. I like to eat everything in sight, and I just can't help it. I'm always super hungry. When I eat a lot, it sometimes makes me have a rumbly belly, which means I can produce some extra smelly things from my little patootie from all the stinky air built up in my belly. It's a small price to pay for all the yummy things I get to eat. One of my favorite foods is mustard. And before you ask the question, YES mustard is a food. It's the best food in fact. And gosh, do I love it so much. I like to put it on anything and everything, and I do mean everything. I like to make bizarre and new combinations with my food, so I will always add mustard on top of anything I eat. My friends and I love to go on adventures together, and we can sometimes get into some crazy situations. But we will get to all of that later.

I have a great group of friends that like to come on adventures with me that I will be introducing to you. My bestest friend in the whole wide world is Seymour the seal. She is just as daring as I am, and she always joins me for all my adventures. She is tiny like me, so we can scurry around together everywhere we go. We do everything together and we always have each other's backs.

Butternuts is a golden retriever puppy and is always ready to have fun. She is usually our voice of reason when Seymour and I get a little carried away. Mr. Dog is the brains of our crew, and he always has such good ideas on what adventures we can take. He is the oldest and wisest of our friends and never leaves home without his sweater on; it's his signature look. Leon is our lion cub buddy and he has lots of energy for our daily adventures. We all make an amazing team and always have the best of times together.

My friends and I all live together in a huge house that has two floors. We start our daily adventures as soon as our human friend Colin goes to school, and his parents go to work. Every morning, we eat breakfast together and decide what kind of adventures we will get into for the day. Mr. Dog and Butternuts are the ones that usually make breakfast since nobody likes mustard in their eggs like I do. I really don't know why they don't like mustard on their eggs! They like to put ketchup on theirs, how gross is that? Mr. Dog loves to make big fluffy pancakes, and I usually make a huge sticky mess of the syrup. Have you ever tried syrup mixed with mustard? If you haven't tried it on top of your pancakes, or waffles,

I highly suggest it since it's so yummy. Once we all have our breakfast and get our bellies nice and full, we can start to plan our daily adventure.

CHAPTER 2

The weather outside today is just perfect. It's hot and sunny and the kind of day you crave in the summertime. There was not a single cloud in the big beautiful blue sky. Today would be a PERFECT day for a barbeque lunch! There is nothing like the yummy smell of barbequed meat and hot dogs cooking on the grill outside. The delicious smells from the grill make my tummy growl every single time. I am getting a rumbly in my tummy right now just thinking about it.

"Hey, friends, I have a great idea for what we can do today!" I said to the bunch at the breakfast table.

"I hope it has something to do with a pool, since it's so hot outside today," said Seymour.

"Yeah, me too!" piped in Mr. Dog.

"It sure does!" I said. "We need to get out the inflatable pool and set it up in the backyard, and then we can do a cookout for lunch. Doesn't that sound perfect?"

"It sure does, except we have one small problem," said Butternuts.

"There is no problem we can't fix if we all work together, Butternuts. What is the problem?" I said.

"We have nothing to grill. Our groceries I ordered online won't be delivered until tomorrow," Butternuts said. "And I don't think a peanut butter and jelly sandwich would taste as good if I grilled it," she added, chuckling. Personally, I think a grilled peanut butter, jelly, and mustard sandwich sounds amazing. But I kept that thought to myself.

"Pshhh, Seymour and I can take our scooters up to the store and pick up a few things for us to grill for lunch. Problem solved!" I said. I love riding around on my scooter. There is nothing better than the fresh warm summer air wafting through my fur. I love to drive my scooter fast down the sidewalk. I make sure I'm extra safe too and always wear my helmet and my paw pads.

Just as I was getting excited to get my scooter out, the doorbell rang. The chime was so loud that I jumped at least one foot in the air, which is high since I'm so tiny. We all looked at each other since we weren't expecting anybody.

"Who could that be?" asked Mr. Dog.

Everyone got up from the table and crowded around the door opening in the kitchen to sneak a peek out the front door. Since I can't see out of the peephole, Mr. Dog went up to the door to see who was there. He peeked through the little peephole and slowly opened the door.

"Hi there, can I help you?" he said.

There stood a friendly looking pooch with a giant platter in his paws; I couldn't tell what was on his platter from where I was standing. There was a big white truck parked in the driveway with a picture of some hotdogs and hamburgers on the side. Just looking at that yummy picture of those burgers and dogs and imagining it

dripping with mustard was making me
start to slobber.

"Hi, mister, my name is Tito and I'm going
door-to-door selling some delicious meat.
I thought it would be the perfect day to drive
around the neighborhood and see if anyone
wants to buy some. I have some pork chops,
some yummy ribs with loads of BBQ sauce,
some hot dogs, and hamburgers, and of
course, some crispy super delicious bacon....
That is my favorite. Here is a sample of each
one if you would like to try some."

The smell of delicious meat wafted into
the kitchen, and I started to drool a little
bit. I just couldn't help myself—the drool
just started flowing out of my mouth. I went
into a meat daze for a second thinking of all
this delicious meat Tito just talked about.

"Did he say he was selling all of this
yummy meat?" I asked. The spirits in food
Heaven have answered my prayers. This
pup just magically appeared asking me and
my friends if we want free samples of meat.
"Hey, I have a great idea—why don't we buy
this right now, so we don't have to go to the
grocery store. Tito the meat salespup needs

to come inside, and we can taste all the meats he has! I hope he brought some extra mustard for dipping!" I exclaimed.

"Yes! That sounds like a perfect plan. But Skunky, please, please, please don't get the mustard out! Every time you do, you make the biggest mess!" said Butternuts. "We don't want you to embarrass yourself in front of our new friend Tito," she added.

"Jeez, Butternuts, you are no fun today!" I said while laughing. "Just kidding — I promise to not make another mustard mess!"

Mr. Dog stood there with his tongue hanging out—he can't resist ribs especially the ones that are dripping in BBQ sauce. I'm pretty sure I saw a couple of drool droplets hit the floor.

"Please come in, Tito, we were just talking about what a perfect day it is outside to have a cookout, and that we had no food to grill. Then here you are. You just appeared with all this meat—it's like magic," said Mr. Dog. "Delicious meaty magic!"

Tito decided to come inside, and he brought all those yummy smells with him.

Before he set his platter of meat down on the kitchen table, everyone went around the table and introduced themselves. Tito sat down the platter and went over each cut of meat individually. It reminded me of when we go out to eat and the nice waitress goes over each single yummy dessert that is on the platter. I started to drool again just thinking about all those desserts. I had to snap out of it since there was this gold mine of meat sitting right in front of me.

"First we have the pork chop," Tito said. "You can get boneless or one with the bone, and these go perfectly on the grill. You can season them or sop them in sauce—they are delicious and juicy any way you cook them. Then we have the ribs, these taste the best when they are dripping in BBQ sauce. They are so tender; they just fall off the bone," Tito said.

I looked at Seymour and we were both drooling all over the place! Our eyes were as big as saucers. A small pool of drool was starting to form on the kitchen table. If Tito doesn't hurry up and finish his speech on all these meats, I am going to go bonkers.

And we will need to get some towels to wipe up my pools of drool.

"Next we have the hot dogs and hamburgers. You can't have a cookout without dogs and burgers, right? I'll even throw in a delicious cheese sampler for you for free. That's right, I said for free!" Tito exclaimed. "Then we have the cream of the crop, the cherry on top, the crispy and ever so yummy BACON. This is my favorite—especially when it's cooked on the grill and is extra crispy! I don't have much of this left since I got hungry in the truck and kind of ate some already." He had a small grin on his face as he thought about how delicious that bacon was this morning. I noticed some tiny bacon crumbs and a greasy sheen in Tito's whiskers. I don't blame him for eating it in the car. If I was a meat sales raccoon, there wouldn't be any meat left to sell. I would have dived right in and sampled it all before I even left the driveway.

"So, what do you say? Do you want to make your cookout fantastic and buy this meat package? I'll give you a super good deal since you all look like a nice crew," Tito said.

Butternuts, Mr. Dog, Leon, Seymour, and I all looked around the table. All of us were slobbering at the sight of this delicious meat platter. Leon replied, "We will take it all! And since you look like you are a fun pooch, why don't you stay over and eat with us. We are going to set up the pool outside and have a super fun day in the backyard. What do you say?"

"Wow, that sounds like fun. Thanks, everyone! Since I already ate most of the bacon, I'll give you a good deal. Sorry about that. I can't control myself when there is crispy delicious bacon lying right beside me," laughed Tito.

Tito left his meat platter on the table and went out to his truck to grab the cooler of meat for all of us. While he was outside, I couldn't help myself and tried a little nibble of the ribs. Oh boy, were they delicious! "Let's get this cookout started before I lose my mind sitting next to all of this meat," I said with drool and slobber spraying out from my mouth.

CHAPTER 3

Leon and Butternuts grabbed the pool from inside the garage and started to drag it to the backyard.

"Be gentle with that you two. I don't want your little choppers puncturing a hole in the pool!" yelled Mr. Dog. He turned on the grill, and I could already smell the scrumptious aroma of barbeque wafting throughout the air. Mr. Dog is a great chef and we put him charge of cooking all this food that Tito brought over. Tito was helping him cook and was telling him what spices and seasonings to put on the pork chops and the hamburgers. He seems to be a great cook too, and I know that both pups together will make this an unforgettable meaty lunch.

"Don't worry, Mr. Dog—we are being super careful with the pool!" yelled back Leon.

They got the pool in the backyard in one piece and went back to get the air pump. Leon plugged it into the outlet they had outside and turned it on. In no time at all, the pool was inflated and ready for the hose and the water. I'm so glad I have so many bigger and stronger friends. It would have been hard for me and Seymour to try and get the pool out ourselves.

Since Mr. Dog and Tito were on the grill, and Leon and Butternuts got the pool out, I figured Seymour and I could oversee filling it up. "Seymour, can you turn on the water so I can fill up the pool?" I yelled out as I was sitting on the edge of the hose. I was able to point the end of the hose into the pool, and I just needed Seymour to slowly turn on the water.

Seymour ran on the top of the water nozzle; she started out slow and the water started to trickle on. But then she lost her footing and started spinning around and around super fast. She couldn't stop and was spinning so fast she looked like a little white furry blur on top of the hose spout. It reminded me of when a hamster spins in their little hamster wheel and goes out of control. I couldn't help but laugh a little bit.

My little chuckle was cut short when the water kicked on full blast.

"*AHHHHHHHHH!*" I yelled. "Turn it off, turn it off!" The hose took on a life of its own, and I was riding it like a bucking bronco trying to hold on for dear life. The water was on the highest setting like a fireman shooting his firehose right out of a fire hydrant. The hose was flailing all over the place with me on it, and the water was shooting out all over the backyard... everywhere except the inside of the pool. "Turn it off, turn it off!" I yelled again.

Butternuts ran over and turned off the nozzle and grabbed Seymour who was super dizzy from her ride. I'm surprised I didn't see those little birdies flying around her head like you see in the cartoons. Once the hose stopped, I couldn't hold on any longer. I started to take flight and was going in the direction of the picnic table. I looked down and saw a most amazing sight, a giant tub of mustard right next to the potato salad. As I started my initial descent, I was very

thankful that Mr. Dog brought out the mustard already and placed it in the spot that he did. "Cannonball" I yelled as I went flying from the hose to the tub of mustard. I made a huge splash as I landed, and mustard went everywhere.

I lifted my head out of the tub and licked all the mustard off my face... *mmmmmmmmm mmmmm* that tasted so good! I really don't understand why my friends don't love mustard like I do. It's the most delicious food ever created! And it goes with everything, and I mean everything!

"Skunky—you got mustard all over the table, and on top of my potato salad," said Mr. Dog.

Oh no, I thought, I really hope he's not mad at me. I couldn't help it this time, I flung off that hose so quick I didn't even have time to think. "Looks like your regular potato salad is now mustard potato salad, Mr. Dog," I said, laughing and licking off the rest of the mustard from my face. "Potato salad is so boring without gobs and gobs of mustard in it," I yelled out so everyone could hear me.

"Oh, Skunky," laughed Mr. Dog. "Can we ever have a day where you don't get into the mustard? Every single day you get into the mustard or have some sort of mustard mishap," he added.

"Apparently not," I said proudly. I really

need to get a bright yellow mustard-colored shirt with the words Mr. Mustard Mishap printed big on it.

Tito helped Butternuts fill the pool since it was clearly too big of a job for Seymour and me to handle. Mr. Dog was just about done with grilling all the meat. "Leon, can you please go inside and grab the fruit salad I made earlier and bring it out to the table? Butternuts, can you please grab the plates and napkins for me?" yelled Mr. Dog.

While the pool was filling up with ice-cold crisp water, the gang all sat down at the picnic table to eat their feast. Mr. Dog did an awesome job cooking up the food, and we all gobbled it down so quick that nobody said a word as they were eating. The food was so good, and Tito and Mr. Dog cooked it all perfectly. I am so glad they know how to cook. If I was in charge, it would be mustard sandwiches every single day. I'm so glad I don't wear pants because if I did, they would be bursting at the seams right about now.

"I think I could use a nice dip in the pool before we get to the dessert. It's so hot and

I need to cool off for a bit," said Seymour. "I'm so full right now I will probably bob around like a tiny beach ball once I get into the pool," she joked.

We all agreed and jumped into the pool. It felt so nice to feel that cold water since the sun had been nonstop since we all woke up that morning. We were all so full and hot from eating our delicious BBQ lunch that a nice cooldown in our pool was just what we all needed. My friends and I just sat there and closed our eyes and relaxed. This is what life is all about, I thought to myself. Having a delicious meal and relaxing with my friends. Nothing could spoil this moment.

CHAPTER 4

We were all sitting in the pool just soaking up the sun and enjoying the cool water and each other's company. Until we heard a loud rumbly sound.

Ggrrrmmmrrrr.

Mr. Dog jolted up from his relaxed daze. "What on earth was that noise?"

Bbrrrrhhhmmmrrrppp.

"There it was again. Did you guys hear that?" asked Mr. Dog

"Yeah, I heard it too. I feel like I've heard that sound before, but I can't pinpoint what it is," said Butternuts.

Oh no, I thought to myself. I just know I had that look on my face. It was a look my friends have witnessed a million times. It was the look that meant either I was about to get into some sort of trouble, or something crazy was about to happen!

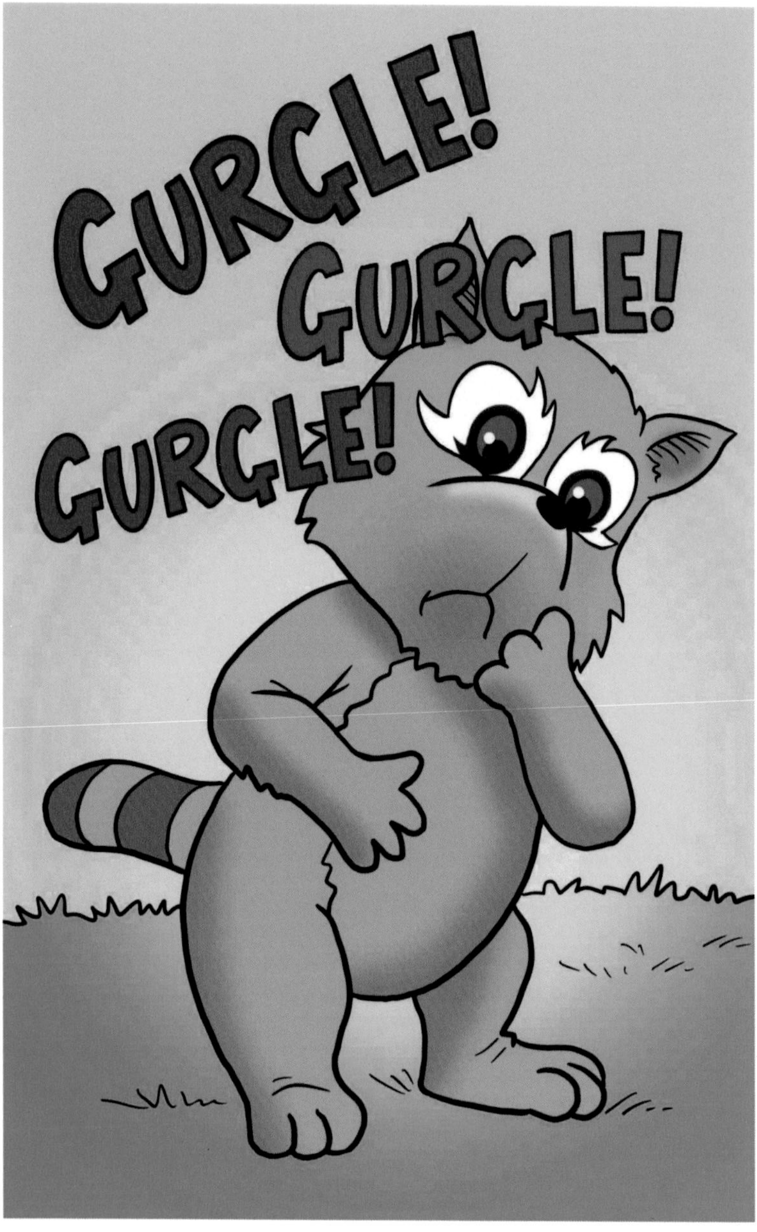
GURGLE!
GURGLE!
GURGLE!

I couldn't deny the look any longer. I had to say something before I burst.

"Um, gang?" I said. "My tummy is feeling a little extra rumbly right now. I should probably get out of the pool. I think I ate a little too much at lunchtime."

"Skunky, what all did you eat for lunch?" Mr. Dog asked. "I was so focused on my delicious plate of food that I didn't even pay attention to what anyone else was eating."

Oh boy, I thought, I really overdid it this time. "Well, I had a hot dog covered in mustard, a cheeseburger covered in mustard, then I had some mustard potato salad, and a big pork chop that I also covered in mustard," I said.

"You ate all of that, Skunky?" Mr. Dog said. "How did you even fit all of that in your tiny little body?"

"Well, no," I said. "I also had some ribs that I dipped in mustard and some fruit salad with a side of mustard. And oh yea, some baked beans that I topped with mustard too. Hmmmm, I think that was it."

Mr. Dog was just shaking his head. "Oh, Skunky," he said.

And just as I started to crawl my way out of the pool that is when it happened. I couldn't hold it in anymore—it was impossible. Was it all the ribs I had? Or all the potato salad and fruit? Or the gobs of mustard I licked up after my lunch was finished? Whatever it was, I knew I was doomed. Totally doomed.

I let out the biggest patootie shriek in the pool and it was epic. It was the king toot of all toots. It was so loud and powerful that it tore a hole in the side of the pool. I was kind of proud of the noise that I created, especially since I'm so tiny. But while I was patting myself on the back, I realized that I needed to get everyone out of the pool. I don't think anyone noticed the little hole that I made from my amazing epic rump hooting.

"AHHHHHH, everyone, you should probably get out of the pool! She's gonna blow!" I yelled.

Everyone scrambled to get out of the pool. I don't know whose nails did the extra damage, but when they scrambled to get out of the pool, there were some extra rips and

tears along the bottom. The air was escaping so quick from the pool—it sounded like a super big horn instrument playing in a symphony. Almost like a tuba sound or maybe even a trumpet. I don't know the horn instruments that well, but all I know is I created this crazy sound with the little toot that came out of my little tiny patootie! The neighbors were probably wondering what on earth we all were doing in our backyard. The water was spraying out so quickly that it was faster than the air escaping. Once most of the water was out of the pool, the pool magically took flight and started flying around like a helium balloon that was let go in the sky. It was making some shrieking noises as it zoomed all around.

We all just stood there and watched our inflatable pool fly around like a crazy bug. It finally landed in the big tree in our backyard. We all stopped and looked at each other, not believing what just happened. Then we all just started cracking up!

"Sorry, guys," I said. "I guess they don't call me Skunky for nothing!" I started laughing out loud; I couldn't help myself.

"You can say that again!" laughed Mr. Dog.

Everyone pitched in to clean up the mess and get the pool down from the tree. With all of us working together, it didn't take that long to clean up. Once that was all done and the yard was sparkling and spotless, we all went inside of our house to relax. Between that fiasco and the big lunch, I was utterly pooped out and ready for a nap.

Another wonderful day and crazy adventure with my friends have come to an end. I am so thankful for each one of my friends and happy that Tito has joined our squad. Despite all the silly things I get into and the mustard mishaps I always seem to have, they always have my back and love me just as much as I love all of them. They are my family and I am grateful to get to go on amazing fun escapades with them every single day.

I can't wait to see what kind of adventures tomorrow will bring!

The End!